MEG UP THE CREEK

for Abigail

MEG up the CREEK

by Helen Nicoll
and Jan Pieńkowski

PUFFIN BOOKS

Meg Mog and Owl went in a canoe

up the creek

and into the wood

Owl and Mog went hunting

Wait for me

wobble

Tally ho!

Half for you half for me

POUNCE

Rats! Too late

And mine

That's mine!

Bon appétit

Owl went to find Meg

Have a blackberry...

What about a mushroom?

There's Mog

They found Mog

Did you catch anything?

Nearly

Lucky I've got something in the cauldron

I'm starving

They rushed back

What is it?

It's a surprise

Smells funny

It's moving

It's alive

EEEK!

It's a...

FOX!

There goes dinner

We'll starve

Oh dear oh dear

It got dark

RUSTLE

I'm cold

They heard strange noises

What's that?

SNAP

BARK

The canoe drifted away

How will we get home?

I think I'll make a spell

RUB RUB

The fire would not light

Meg put in

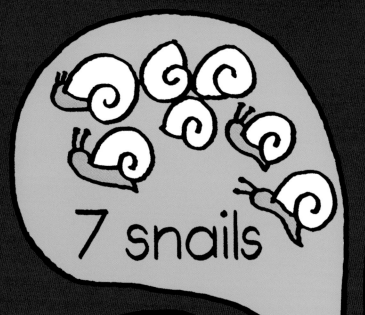

7 snails

4 fire flies

a bird's nest

and a snap dragon

Fire! Fire!
Strike a light
Flash bang wallop
Get a fright

and she made her spell

It went like a rocket

FIZZ WHEEE

You called?

Have you got a match?

The fire lit

They all had supper

There's a feather in my soup

Can I have some more?

You must come to stay

I hope he doesn't stay too long

There's our house

What's for tea?

They all flew home

Goodbye!